The Adventures of Robbie Rabbit And Rando Racoon

Written by Phyllis Heinly
Illustrated by Carol Coulson

Copyright © 2021 by Phyllis Heinly

All rights reserved. No part of this publication may be reproduced, distributed, or transmitted in any form or by any means, including photocopying, recording, or other electronic or mechanical methods, without the prior written permission of the publisher, except in the case brief quotations embodied in critical reviews and other noncommercial uses permitted by copyright law.

ISBN: 978-1-63945-297-2 (Paperback)
        978-1-63945-298-9 (E-book)

The views expressed in this book are solely those of the author and do not necessarily reflect the views of the publisher, and the publisher hereby disclaims any responsibility for them.

Writers' Branding
1800-608-6550
www.writersbranding.com
orders@writersbranding.com

Dedicated to all the wonderful pets I have had throughout my life.

Robbie Rabbit hopped as fast as he could from the field into the darkened town, he must find a place to hide. He could hear the howling of the hounds just a short distance behind him and finding a safe haven was of the utmost importance. Racing down the main street, he spied a vacant building at the end of a long alley. Thinking he might find cover there, he moved as fast as he could toward the building. Soon, he found a crack just big enough for his little body to slip through, he squeezed into the empty room shaking with fright. The dogs ran past never suspecting that Robbie was hiding only a few feet away on the very street they were searching.

Robbie did not move for the longest time waiting, listening, and being very careful not to give away his hiding place. After a while, he began to relax and as his eyes adjusted to the darkness, he became aware of the dilapidated condition of the room. Robbie could tell that no one had been working here for a long time. Dust and cobwebs were everywhere and furniture was crumbling with age. While he was hopping around checking out his surroundings, Robbie thought he heard a loud sneeze.

Suddenly, a closet door flew open and out rolled a small dark animal. His eyes were very bright and Robbie could see them plainly through the darkness. It was Rando Raccoon. They had been friends for years, and upon realizing, they had both picked the same building to hide in, they just rolled around laughing and hugging.

Their surprise meeting led to a joyous conversation of the goings on in their lives since they had last met. And so, the clear, cool evening passed quickly while the hounds continued circling the fields outside of town looking for the two of them. After staying awake all night talking, the two friends were really exhausted by dawn. Nevertheless, they felt the safest thing to do would be to part and try making it to their homes. After a brief rest, they planned to meet again in a few weeks and travel together around the countryside looking for adventure.

So, on a bright sunny day, Robbie Rabbit and Rando Raccoon joined up again to begin their adventures traveling around the countryside. The memory of the hounds had long passed and they were anxiously looking forward to the new day.

Robbie and Rando had been on the road for many weeks. They did a lot of sightseeing but nothing extraordinary happened along the way until one morning. It was just before dawn; they had been sleeping in an old hollow log for protection and warmth.

Suddenly, they were thrown side to side and up and down and finally flew through the air and landed on the soft pine needles a few feet away from each other. After rubbing their eyes, they looked up from where they lay and saw, to their surprise, a huge brown bear. The bear was looking for something to eat and did not even see the two little travelers fly out of the log. Quickly, Robbie and Rando rolled over behind a large gray rock to hide. They remained there and watched as the bear continued to rummage through the underbrush nearby. Suddenly, the bear started to jump around and let out little yelps. Then he fell to the ground with a loud thud. Something was terribly wrong. Robbie and Rando peeked out from behind the rock and saw the bear remained on the ground in the same place yelping, growling, and roaring at the top of his lungs.

Cautiously, the two crept up to the bear where they could examine the problem more closely. It was a trap, yes, a spring trap, one that was set in the forest to catch some unsuspecting animal. They felt bad for the bear, but what could they do? Quietly, they discussed the situation. Somehow, they had to free him from the rope that had tangled around his ankle. Their claws alone were not sharp enough to cut through the very thick twine. After a few minutes, Robbie said to Rando, "Let me see your teeth." After examining the sharpness of Rando's teeth, Robbie suggested that he chew through the twine and set the big bear free. So, that is exactly what Rando did and within minutes, she had chewed enough of the rope to weaken it. Then the bear made one enormous heave and broke the rope. Now, the bear stood up. He was released from danger. Looking around, the bear's eyes fell on the two little travelers. "Thank you, thank you," he said, picking them up in his big hairy arms. He hugged them and hugged them. Now they were friends, Robbie and Rando told the bear that they were just traveling around for adventure and asked if he would like to join them. The bear told them he could not because he had family back in the more dense part of the woods and had to find food and take care of them. He told them he hoped they would stay safe and have lots of fun, then they said their good-byes.

THE METEOR

Robbie and Rando were determined to continue their travels even though they missed their families. They were thinking about the stories they would be able to tell everyone when they got back. This would more than make up for time spent away from loved ones.

The night was clear as a bell and the reflection of the half-moon glistened on the lake where they had made their campsite for the night. They sat around a fire made to cook and keep warm. Rando was roasting a couple of grubs over the fire for a delicious supper while Robbie was munching on some fresh and tender blades of grass nearby. It was another enjoyable evening. After eating they settled down for sleep. As they said their good nights, something huge and bright shot across the sky. Robbie told Rando he thought it might have been a meteor. They took note of the area where it might have hit the earth. Rando said that he remembered stories told when he was young about meteors cracking open when they hit the earth. Inside, they were filled with gold and precious stones. A thought came to both of the little animals at the same time. Tomorrow, they would hike to the area where they suspected the meteor might have hit the earth and explore. Maybe they would get lucky and find a treasure.

The next morning, they were up and on the way through the woods before sunrise. It was exciting to think they might find the actual spot where the meteor hit and see wonderful things. The weather was pleasant that day with bright sun, a soft breeze, and plenty of food along the way. They traveled for miles toward their goal, but the first day brought no results. They camped for the night hoping for better luck the next day.

The little animals slept late the next morning because they were very tired from their long walk the day before. Soon, they were on their way again hiking through the woods and singing a little song to pass the time. About two hours into their walk, Rando noticed the top of some of the trees they were passing under were broken off. He mentioned this to Robbie, who then looked up and also saw the broken treetops. Now they knew they were headed in the right direction and continued to follow the broken treetops. Soon, they came to an area where all the ground was darkened, as if by a fire and there it was, the meteor. Not much was left of the meteor by the time it hit the earth. What remained was not the gold and precious gems the two had hoped to find but purple, white, aqua, and black rock shining beautifully in the bright sunshine.

That night, they camped there next to where the meteor had hit the earth. Although they had not found a treasure inside the meteor, the fact remained that they were the first and would maybe be the only ones ever to see this meteor and that made them very happy.

The next morning when they awoke, Rando with his expert paws, began to collect a few of the shiny rock pieces that were laying around the meteor. Robbie helped him put the rocks into one of the backpacks they had with them. By now, these shiny stones had become precious to them, the needed proof to show their families when they told everyone about their discovery in the forest.

Filling the bag was hard work for Robbie and Rando. When they were finished, they ate a small meal and settled down for another night in the forest with dreams of what would be their next adventure.